Written by Brad Scott
Cover art by Brad Scott
Concept art by Brad Scott

Editors:
Steffanie Moyers
Gerladine Nyika
Paula Woulas

Published by Brad Scott Studios

ISBN 979-8-9862134-0-8

Special Thanks to:
Jennifer Perkins
Carson Jeffries
Kool As Heck
Brian Lue Sang
Paula Woulas
Jason Woulas
Peter Pappas
My Family

Special Acknowledgements to:
Blender.org
KitBash3D.com
FantasyNameGenerators.com

VAPOR

by
Brad Scott

The year is 258 EE. A little more than 258 years after the Earth Evacuation. The inhabitants of earth have established colonies in the Cerulis district of the Virgo Supercluster, post the meteor strike that rendered earth uninhabitable. A few small planets in the galaxy have been discovered that sustain carbon life forms. Advanced Renewable Energy Systems (ARES) provide reliable power to the planets, but water is the limitation factor. Due to the lack of water, livestock is highly regulated and vegetables are the staple food. The habitable planets yield very little water, so water vapor is mined from clouds found in the expanse that exists between celestial bodies. Water barons control the flow of water, and space lanes are filled with cargo ships, mercenaries, and pirates. All in the search for vapor.

"Vapor" explores the intersecting lives of space captains, as humanity struggles to exist in unknown worlds.

Vapor
Episode 1

Second Sun

Deep space travel is peaceful to some and maddening to others. The quiet, the darkness, the isolation. Captain Jons enjoyed the isolation. As he stood at the helm of his Class 9 cargo ship, the Prophecy, he looked out over the floating spheres and streaks of light, imagining the constellations in a dance reminiscent of his high school days. Lost in his thoughts, Jons stood as an imposing figure, measuring a full 2 meters of lean muscle. Though he was on the younger side, too young for a ship captain, Jons' crew respected him fully, many looking at him as a father or big brother.

First Mate Yu served with Jons for almost 2 decades. Together they explored multiple territories and provinces throughout the galaxy. Yu, who also enjoyed deep space travel, could typically read Jons' mind without having to converse with him. Although smaller in stature, most of the crew was deathly afraid of Yu. Yu was resilient and no-nonsense. He knew the horrors of poor practices in space travel and did not stand for such things in the crew. Typically stoic, Yu was also good-humored, and could be brought to laughter with a good joke.

"Another beautiful night, Captain," Yu said calmly as he sided up to Jons.

"Each more beautiful than the other...in their own way," Jons replied.

"Our heading is true and we are about..."

"Don't tell me, Yu." Jons said quietly, "We will get there when we get there."

"Roger that, sir."

And with that, the two shipmates quietly stared out the window as the ship glided through the low density of space.

After about 20 minutes, Second Mate Faaya exclaimed, "Second sun rising, deploy ARES for a tertiary charge."

Faaya's voice was soft but commanding as she controlled the helm.

The order was repeated twice on the bridge and once over the ship's intercom. A voice came back over the radio "Deploying ARES for tertiary charge."

"Slow to charge speed," Faaya commanded.

The order was repeated twice on the bridge, and a voice came back from across the room, "Slowing to charge speed."

It was like that on the Prophecy. Orders were repeated and acknowledged as clockwork. Not just for tradition, but for the safety of the crew and the spacecraft. By repeating orders for all to hear, mistakes were minimized.

Prophecy slowed its speed as solar panels were discharged from the lower bays to catch the rising second sun. This far out in space, sunlight made two appearances. The main sun rose high above the horizon of a far-off planet and lasted for several hours. The second sun barely broke daylight and only lasted about one hour. But without the interference of clouds and thick atmospheres, the second sun was bright and made for a good top off of the ARES.

As the sun began to break the horizon, Watch Leader Leandro shouted across the bridge, "Vessel at 5 o'clock high!"

Jons looked out over the bridge capsule and then the radar. "Why are they not showing on our radar?"

Yu looked at the Engineering section, "Systems check."

"All systems go," a puzzled voice came back.

"They had to be back there for a while, Captain. It was not noticeable until it was illuminated by the sun," announced Leandro.

"Any distress signals?" Yu asked, eyeing the C5 Center.

"Scanning all channels; no signals detected," stated the Command, Control, Communication, Computers, and Cyber section.

Captain Jons felt his hands slowly tighten to fists, "Pop flare."

"Pop flare," the command was repeated and executed on the bridge.

From the top of the spacecraft, a flare shot several hundred meters into the air and then exploded into a bright starburst of green and yellow. Spacecraft had adapted to using flares versus flags for ship identifiers, as flares can be readily seen in the darkness of space. There was a long pause, which seemed to last beyond the customary response time. From the vessel on the horizon a stream of smoke appeared as a flare rose above its deck and burst into a flickering display of red and yellow.

"FIRE FLARE!" yelled Watch Leader Leandro.

"Pirates," Jons said softly, only loud enough for Yu to hear, but everyone on board knew the fire flare was the symbol for pirates. In deep space, black flags and black flares cannot be seen, so pirates adopted the fire flare as their symbol.

Jons moved with a purpose and began giving orders in rapid succession.

"I have the conn."

"Capt'n has the conn," Second Mate Faaya yielded control of the ship.

"Retract the ARES, increase speed to 90%, make your heading 350 degrees, 5 degrees down bubble."

All orders were repeated and executed precisely as Yu had trained the crew.

Jons picked up the ship's microphone, clicking to ship-wide mode, "Attention on deck, pirates in pursuit, deploy weapons, seal bulkheads, and attend battle stations. Prepare to be boarded."

"Boarded sir?" a voice came from across the bridge.

"Yes. We have a ship full of vapor and will not be able to outrun it. The best thing we can do is to bide our time and prepare for a fight."

"Roger that, Captain."

"Chief Jebel, ready the bridge for hand-to-hand combat."

"Yes, Captain."

"First Mate Yu."

"Yes, Captain."

"Bring the fury."

"Aye, aye, Captain."

###

A short distance away…

"Captain, the second sun will be rising soon." First Mate Vincent stated in a matter-of-fact and calm voice.

"Ready the ARES for full power and level off at 8,000 meters above their deck," replied Captain Bergon.

Bergon continued, "Continue blackout and ready the crew for aggressive maneuvers."

These orders were not repeated by the crew, but executed with precision none the less.

Captain Xavier Bergon and First Mate Mercy Vincent were like brothers. They have flown together since they were both caught as stowaways aboard a Class 3 Frigate over 30 years ago. By happenstance, they had both simultaneously ditched grade school to explore a life of adventure. Both were found by the frigate crew and brought to the ship's court for discipline and sentenced to hard labor aboard the frigate for the 2-year journey. Surprisingly, neither boy cared about the sentencing and worked harder than many of the paid crew. Both boys were young, but big for their age. Although one year younger, Bergon was a natural leader and Vincent seconded him without contention. After the 2-year sentence was up and the frigate returned to land dock, the boys asked Captain Middleton to extend their sentence in order for them to return to space. The captain denied their request, but instead offered them low positions among the crew. The boys eagerly accepted without a second thought.

After more than a decade aboard the frigate, Captain Middleton explained to the boys, now young men, that he had nothing more to teach them, and sold their contracts to a Class 1 Carrier. Above the carrier, Bergon and Vincent learned to fly just about everything in the space inventory. For a time, they were even fighter pilots assigned to escort duty for various cargo and diplomatic missions. When a series of unfortunate events lead them to a life of pirating, they quickly became a notorious bane of the firmament.

"Commander U, standby for full throttle," Captain Bergon stated with anticipation.

"Aye, Aye, Captain." Replied Commander Rosa Unadóttir, Commander U for short.

Rosa was a highly skilled pilot recruited by Bergon and Vincent more than 15 years ago. She could steer a spaceship by feel, requiring no radar or instrumentation. She had honed her skills as a Class 5 Command Ship pilot in the military. During combat maneuvers, she would steer her command vessel in and around battlefields, providing her leadership with unparalleled views of the combat zone. She remained thankful and loyal to Bergon and Vincent since they were the first to assign such high-profile duties to a female pilot.

The ship's bridge was quiet as the crew stood ready. They had been here before and knew the next few minutes would determine the next few hours.

"Standby for second sun!" exclaimed Second Mate Wells, the ship's navigator.

"Easy, Wells." Captain Bergon urged, "We're not there yet."

Time seemed to stand still as the crew watched the sun crest the horizon, highlighting the ship below them to their left. Several members of the crew leaned in toward their video screens and radar units. Then it appeared, a flare released from the ship below and exploded into a green and yellow starburst right in front of their eyes.

"Now, Captain?" asked Adrian Rey, the ship's communication's officer.

"Not yet, Rey. I want them to sweat a minute." Bergon counted to an arbitrary number in his head and then just shouted, "Now!"

Rey released a flare from the Black Dagger, which flickered into a bright red and yellow display against the low sun. The Black Dagger was a highly modified Class 2 Destroyer. After years in space and aboard every type of vehicle imaginable, Bergon and

Vincent designed a craft that was fast and agile, yet capable of extended stints away from port. The Black Dagger also housed an array of gadgetry that could be configured to carry a variety of loads.

Once the flare ignited, Commander Unadóttir immediately began pushing the throttle forward and steering Black Dagger towards the Prophecy. The boarding crew was already in their spacesuits and armed for close quarters combat (CQC).

"Open all comm channels," Bergon stated.

"All channels open Capt'n," replied Second Mate Rey.

"This is Captain Bergon of the Black Dagger. I am sure you are familiar with our ship, so I will cut to the meat of it all. We are here for your cargo, not your lives. My crew and I don't have families. We have neither lives in the colonies nor a spaceport to rendezvous with. Our mission is simple: we steal, sell, and enjoy the splendors of life. Stop your ship and provide us with half your load and we will be on our way. Resist, and your crew will pay the ultimate price. I urge you to take our offer seriously and return to your homes, families, and friends."

"This is Captain Jons of the Prophecy. We are a civilian merchant ship carrying vapor for the settlements. We must supply three colonies; therefore, we cannot provide you with half our load. However, we are willing to ensure you have enough vapor to sustain yourselves. What say you?"

"Captain Jons. I respect your position, but I must insist on half your load."

"Very well, Captain Bergon. My crew will be ready to receive you with mayhem. Prophecy out."

###

"Commander U, how long until intercept?"

"15 minutes, Captain Bergon."

"Make it 12."

"Aye, sir."

###

"Captain Jons, 15 minutes till they reach our destination."

"Thank you, Second Mate Faaya."

T-15

Fifteen minutes till intercept and the Black Dagger crew is relaxed and jovial. The boarding crew stands ready in the airlock with spacesuits on and helmets in hand. They are armed with compact rifles, pistols, and pulaskis. The rifles are loaded with rapid-fire low-velocity projectile (LVP) rounds designed for indoor combat. The rounds are ideal for low gravity trajectory with enough speed to puncture clothing and flesh, but not powerful enough to damage metal or tempered glass. Space vehicle combat is dangerous enough without the threat of creating a vacuum due to an errant shot. The pistols contain small dart-like projectiles and carry tranquilizer fluid. The needles are strong, small, and can puncture space suits with a sealant on the end to prevent air loss. This disables the victim without compromising their spacesuits. The pulaskis are custom-made, non-sparking, stainless steel. One end of the pulaski combines an axe and an adze, while the other end is fashioned into a 3-blade fixed broadhead spear. The pulaski is used for breaching, cutting, ripping, chopping, and close quarters combat (CQC).

"Make sure your air is on this time, Jonas."

"Yeah, Blaine, did you pee this time before we loaded up?"

"Oh, you go to hell."

"I'm in hell everyday with you on this ship."

The Back Dagger boarding crew jokes with each other while performing last-minute equipment checks. Once the airlock is open, any mistakes can be detrimental to the mission and the crew. But the Black Dagger boarding crew routinely space-walks to maintain proficiency and familiarity with the equipment and the environment.

Aboard the Prophecy, First Mate Yu readied the spacewalk team, as well as, the repel team. In the airlock, Yu performs an equipment check on each member as he issues instructions.

"When the airlock opens, check your air supply and suit pressure before going through the hatch. Once outside, tether to the guide rail and spread out. In order to take the ship, they will have to send over a boarding crew. You kick their ass into space by whatever means possible. If we can keep them out of the airlock, there's no way for them to board the ship. Copy?"

"Aye, aye, sir." the group exclaims.

Yu moves into the main hull and secures the primary airlock hatch. Through the viewing pane he shoots the spacewalk team a thumbs up and six thumbs are returned.

Yu depresses the intercom button on the door security panel and announces "Decompression commencing."

Fans begin to whirl and within a few seconds a yellow light above the door glows as a green light turns off. Yu pushes another button and the exterior airlock doors twist open, and the light above the door changes from yellow to red. The spacewalk crew performs a series of short checks and then begins to exit the door. Once the last member is through the door, Yu closes the exterior door, the yellow light comes on, and he turns his attention to the repel crew.

"The Black Dagger crew is a very proficient pirating crew. Their reputation precedes them, I'm sure for good reason. I suspect they will devise some method of entering the airlock and securing it from their side. At that point, you will only have a few seconds to act appropriately. If they open the interior door without securing the exterior door you could be sucked out into space and suffocate. So, helmets on and tethers secured to the wall. If they secure the exterior door before opening the interior door, remove your tethers and rush the door. Put them down, and put them down hard and fast. Copy?"

"Aye, aye, sir." the group exclaims.

Yu moves to the end of the hallway to address a lone crewman.

"You son, are the failsafe. If the Black Dagger crew gets past the spacewalkers and the repel team, I want you to override the system and open both airlock doors. Hopefully we can surprise them with a little space air as a last resort. If they stay intact and get to this door, move into the main cabin with the rest of the crew and prepare for a full-on assault. You ready?"

"Ready, sir."

T-10

"Captain Jons, the Black Dagger has increased speed. Intercept in seven minutes, not ten," Second Mate Faaya exclaims.

"Shite!" Jons responds as he turns to address his First Mate that has just arrived on deck, "Mr. Yu, is everything ready?"

"Yes, Captain. I assume the Black Dagger will send over a boarding team to secure the hatch, so I have prepared three points of conflict. However, if the legends hold any bit of truth, we need to prepare for a battle on the bridge. Tales of Captain Bergon extol him as a worthy adversary."

"Indeed, Mr. Yu. Indeed."

###

"Captain Bergon, intercept in seven minutes. We will be in distance for cable shots in five."

"Excellent, Commander U. I am heading to the airlock; First Mate Vincent take the helm."

"Ayer, aye, Captain. Vincent has the conn."

With that, Bergon moved expeditiously to the airlock. His spacesuit was already on and he had his helmet in his hands. Bergon was armed with a pistol loaded with an extended clip of LVP rounds and modified rapid-fire capability. He also carried multiple knives and a sword. The sword was primarily ceremonial in nature, identifying him as the captain of the Black Dagger. It was a beautiful triple black sword with a black hilt, blade, and scabbard.

The hilt was utilitarian with a simple design and crafted for easy handling during combat. The blade was black carbon fiber over sharp stainless steel making the blade strong and deadly. The scabbard, however, was functional and decorative. Molded primarily from carbon fiber, the scabbard interior was a mixture of stainless steel and leather which sharpened and cleaned the blade with every withdrawal and placement. The exterior was ornate with precious stones and decorative patterns stitched into the leather wraps. The scabbard also contained a small leather pouch that held another black dagger which could be easily withdrawn for dual-handed combat.

Upon arrival at the airlock, the Black Dagger crew immediately surrendered their attention to Captain Bergon.

"Ladies and gentlemen, it's time to make friends," Captain Bergon said as his upper lip began twitching, a sign the crew recognized as a silent battle cry.

The crew stood up and began running the systems checks with ultra-precision. With each procedural step along the way, their faces began to change as the smiles melted away only to be replaced with looks of disdain. As if to say, how dare they challenge us. As the checks were completed, the crew placed their helmets on, turned on their air supplies, depressurized the airlock, and opened the hatch. No other word was spoken. Not another laugh was uttered.

T-5

"Captain Jons, the Black Dagger is much too fast for us to evade."

"We knew that going in, Faaya. Our goal was not evasion, just buying time."

"Captain, I'm seeing spacewalkers disembark the Black Dagger," Yu said with a puzzled look.

"What?" replied Jons as he rushed to view a video monitor. "Put camera 36 on the big screen."

"Placing camera 36 on the big screen," came a reply from the C5 section.

"What the hell are they planning?" Jons asked himself.

Jons and Yu both moved toward the big screen, in silence and unknowingly in lock-step.

"Yu, I've never seen this approach before. It seems too early for their crew to be outside the cabin already."

"I agree, sir. I don't think they can catch us at this speed with their jetpacks. It's extremely dangerous to even attempt such a maneuver."

"I feel like we are playing right into their hands, my friend. We need to do something completely erratic." After a second of contemplation, Captain Jons yelled, "Reduce speed to zero, roll ship to negative 30 degrees!"

The Prophecy began a space stall and rolled counterclockwise. The Prophecy spacewalker team felt the spacecraft jerk beneath them as their feet lifted away. Moments later they felt another jerk and their tethers snapped taunts, keeping them connected to the Prophecy.

###

"First Mate Vincent, we are coming up on range."

"Roger that, Commander U. Make your final approach, open port side grappling doors, and prepare for mating."

Unadóttir flipped a few switches and heavy metal doors on the port side of the Black Dagger slid open, unnoticeably changing the profile of the Black Dagger. Inside the bay doors were large metal plates that filled the entire opening, revealing no contents on the inside. She then grabbed the steering joystick and pushed it down and to the left while simultaneously adjusting the throttle. The Black Dagger responded instantaneously and began slipping through space sideways while still gaining on the Prophecy.

The Black Dagger crew watched silently as Unadóttir piloted the Black Dagger. Watching her was like trying to catch the secrets of a magician.

"What the hell!" exclaimed Unadóttir.

"What is it, Commander?" replied Vincent.

No reply was given as the entire crew on the bridge of the Black Dagger saw the Prophecy stopping and rolling its hardened hull toward the Black Dagger. At these speeds, an impact at the wrong angle could crumple or even puncture the bow of the Black Dagger. Commander Unadóttir was an expert combat pilot, trained in tight battle spaces with multiple ships and tons of flying debris. She gave way to her combat instincts as her hands danced a choreographed masterpiece across the console. Stick, throttle, button, throttle, switch, stick, throttle. The Black Dagger slowed, rolled, dipped, and came up on the starboard side of the Prophecy, just as she had planned in the first place.

###

"Brace for impact!" Jons yelled across the bridge of the Prophecy and the crew grabbed brace bars at their stations.

But the impact never came. Jons and Yu watched as the Black Dagger performed incredible aerial maneuvers, avoided impact, and then rose along their starboard side.

Shocked, Jons remarked, "How the hell did they do that?"

"Sir, it appears the rumors so far are true." Yu answered.

###

"Release port side grapplers." Vincent ordered.

Upon this command, Unadóttir flipped a hat switch on the console and triggered a toggle that propelled large steel plates from the Black Dagger, attached with heavy cables which unspooled toward the Prophecy.

"Engage magnets." Vincent commanded and the large steel plates became magnetized and slammed against the hull of the Prophecy.

The boarding crew, led by Bergon, attached lanyards to the grappling cables on the port side of the Black Dagger and quickly began scaling toward the Prophecy.

Jons, Yu, and the bridge crew of the Prophecy watched camera 36 as large steel plates began hurling toward their ship. The plates landed with a thud that echoed throughout the Prophecy bulkheads. On camera 36 the bridge crew could see large cables anchoring the Black Dagger to the Prophecy, followed by no less than a dozen pirates.

T-0

Bergon and the Black Dagger crew landed on the hull of the Prophecy and detached their safety lanyards. Swiftly and carefully, they began scaling the hull of the Prophecy, heading toward the main deck. This was the most dangerous part of the mission because the boarding crew was completely untethered at this point. One wrong move could send them floating away into deep space. Most other pirate crews used jet packs as a backup safety system. However, Bergon found those crews to be sloppy and slow with such a crutch. He and Vincent trained the Black Dagger crew to operate independently of tethers and jet packs.

As they crested the deck of the Prophecy, they were met instantaneously by the Prophecy spacewalkers. The Prophecy crew, armed with short spears, began stabbing at the boarding crew, trying to puncture the Black Dagger spacesuits. One spear found its target on the leg of a Black Dagger boarding crew member. The victim stepped back several steps and retrieved a roll of tape from his left side cargo pouch. He quickly tore off a strip, sealed the spacesuit leak, stowed the tape and rejoined the fight. The maneuver was executed calmly and with precision, as if rehearsed 1000 times.

The Black Dagger crew withdrew their pulaskis and engaged the spacewalkers. It became obvious to the Prophecy bridge watching on cameras 36 through

40 that they were outclassed in hand-to-hand combat. The Black Dagger crew parried spear thrusts and punched and kicked the spacewalkers across the deck of the Prophecy. They used their pulaskis like extensions to their own limbs, while taking care not to puncture the suits of the spacewalkers. Instead, they targeted the tethers and sliced them into ribbons. Becoming untethered caused the Prophecy spacewalkers to momentarily freak out, opening them up for a swift kick to send them floating off into space. As the Black Dagger boarding crew watched one-by-one, lights began blinking in the distance as the spacewalkers turned on their rescue beacons. With no more resistance on the deck, the boarding crew turned their attention to the airlock.

Airlocks are notoriously difficult to force open. This was by design since the safety of the ship depended on a good seal. The airlock was reinforced and attached to a reinforced bulkhead. Breaking through was possible, but required a lot of time. Time the Black Dagger did not have. They were sure by now the Prophecy bridge was sending out a distress call. A nearby friendly, or worse yet, an air marshal could already be on its way. These facts were not wasted on the Black Dagger boarding crew. They did not waste their time trying to pry open the airlock seal to cut through the deadbolts. Instead, they turned their attention to approximately 1 meter past the hinges of the airlock frame. That was the sweet spot. Metal skin between bulkheads.

The Black Dagger now anchored their lanyards to the Prophecy and put their pulaskis to work. The stainless steel tools began to dent and ding the spacecraft's skin, deforming it with every blow. After about 10 minutes a small tear appeared, followed by a glint of light and a hissing of air.

###

Aboard the Prophecy, the crew was getting antsy. It had been several years since the last pirate attack. It's been almost a decade. Captain Jons and the bridge crew watched as the pirates defeated their spacewalkers.

"What the hell, they're kicking them off the ship!" exclaimed a young comms officer.

"Exactly as we wanted to do to them," replied First Mate Yu.

Yu and Jons watched as the last spacewalker was kicked into space.

"Begin tracking all rescue devices," Jons ordered.

"Tracking all rescue devices," came a reply from the C5 section.

The radar screen lit up with bleeps from all directions.

"Shite their good," Jons thought to himself.

"I'm going to join the repel team, sir." Yu stated, almost as a matter of fact and not a request for permission. Yet a reply came, nonetheless.

"Roger that, Yu." Jons replied and gave his friend a small head nod.

Yu found the repel team anxious and on edge. Their eyes fixated on the airlock.

"They are tearing through the ship's skin, so helmets on," Yu commanded.

He wanted to tell them to remove their tethers for more freedom of movement, but now he had seen the fighting skills of the Black Dagger crew. He knew the tethers wouldn't make a difference. So instead, he had every other team member attach to the other side of the hall, and then extended everyone in a crisscross pattern. He calculated this would prevent the Black Dagger crew from rushing through as they fought through the repel team.

A few minutes after Yu's arrival in the main hall, the Black Dagger boarding crew was through the side-wall of the main airlock. No longer pressurized, the door to the main hall was locked with a red warning light blinking above.

Unfortunately for the Black Dagger crew, this second door hatch had to be dealt with directly. There was no access to a side wall due to the narrow space. But the boarding crew was prepared. The second door hatch had a digital keypad lock which could be overridden with the proper code. The point man on the boarding crew stepped forward and inserted a digital card into the keypad slot and began running a program on his handheld device. Moments later the second airlock door opened and the Black Dagger crew stepped forward into the main hall to meet the Prophecy crew face-to-face.

The Prophecy crew did not have to wait long. The first Black Dagger crew member through the airlock door immediately engaged the Prophecy defenders. Due to the air rush through the open airlock, the Prophecy crew was slightly disoriented and the first few members went down easy. Black Dagger aggressors struck them in the knee joints and head, taking them out of the fight. By the time the defenders found their equilibrium, they were heavily engaged by the Black Dagger boarding party.

As Captain Bergon walked through the airlock door, he was easily distinguishable as the person in charge. He stood a tall opposing figure, with a strong gait and confident fighting style. The defenders outnumbered the aggressors and the crisscrossing tethers made navigating the hallway difficult. Yu had made a good call on a last-minute tactic. The defenders started to gain the upper hand by overwhelming the aggressors by force in numbers.

Once Bergon noticed a few members of the Black Dagger crew go down, he simply yelled "Now!"

None of the Prophecy had noticed that one member of the Black Dagger crew had remained in the airlock, the locksmith. The locksmith punched a button on his handheld device and the second airlock door rapidly closed. This sudden change in pressure and gravity caught the Prophecy defenders by surprise as most of them fell to the floor. The Black Dagger aggressors understood the command and sequence of events and maintained their footing. The aggressors pounced on the defenders, rendering them unconscious and maimed. Bergon stripped off his helmet as his eyes found 1st Mate Yu. Yu slowly removed his helmet and stared Bergon in the face, raising his weapon to his chest and nodding at the unwelcome pirate captain.

Bergon pushed past his crew and stepped over the broken bodies of the Prophecy crew. His blade sliced through their tethers, creating a clear path for any followers. The few Prophecy members that stepped forward to challenge him were dispatched with little effort.

As Bergon approached, Yu calmly stated "You will not find me so easily bypassed."

Bergon did not reply with words but struck down hard with his pulaski. Yu blocked the overhead strike with a two-arm brace against his spear. He could feel the power of the invading captain, but his will was not shaken. Yu countered triple alternating blows of his spear, nearly finding Bergon's shoulder with the third strike. Bergon realized Yu was a trained fighter as he gathered himself for another attack. Bergon slid left to avoid a third strike, spinning his pulaski in his right hand around Yu's spear to deliver a well-placed blow to Yu's side. Yu, realizing he could not avoid the swing, stepped closer to Bergon to avoid the sharp end of the pulaski and took a blow from the shaft to the ribs. The move was a combination of finesse and force and Yu felt one of his floating ribs crack.

Yu absorbed a hit from Bergon and used the momentum to spin around with a low leg sweep. Bergon tried to sidestep the maneuver, but his movement was interfered with by a fallen defender. A leg sweep caught Bergon on the calf and caused him to go off-balance. He did not fall completely but went down onto one-knee. Both men were now in squatting positions and Yu used the moment to lunge at Bergon. A skilled hand-to-hand fighter, Yu did not recognize his mistake. He was able to tackle Bergon, but his long spear was not effective at this close range. Bergon's pulaski however was still a viable weapon. Bergon jabbed the dagger tip of the pulaski into Yu's thigh enabling him to reverse their position and end up on top of Yu. Bergon maneuvered a knee on top of Yu's spear arm and then stabbed Yu in the opposite arm. Keeping the pulaski driven into Yu's bicep, Bergon reached back and pulled a dagger from his scabbard and stabbed Yu in the forearm, causing Yu to immediately release the spear. Bergon then leaned forward and head-butted Yu right in the nose, resulting in a loud crunch and spray of blood across Yu's face.

As Bergon stood up to examine Yu's mangled body, his crew was clearing the halls of the remaining defenders. Bergon pulled Yu to his feet and walked him to the door at the end of the hall. He looked through the viewing pane of the door to see a Prophecy crew member standing nervously.

"Open this door or I will kill your officer." Bergon commanded.

Yu was dazed and bloody. He wanted to say something, but only blood fell out of his mouth as he attempted to talk. He barely knew where he was. The young crew member stared at Yu, then at Bergon, and back to Yu. His hand slowly reached forward and the hallway door opened.

"Good choice young man. You now have a chance to be a hero and save the life of an officer. Take me to the bridge. Now!"

Captain-to-Captain

The crewman escorted Captain Bergon and his crew to the ship's bridge. Captain Jons had seen the entire battle on the viewing monitors and was ready to receive Bergon. The bridge door was open and Bergon walked in holding Yu up by his collar. Three Black Dagger crew members stepped onto the bridge with Bergon, while the rest remained on alert in the hallway.

"Captain Jons," Bergon stated very congenially. Jons stepped forward and replied "Captain Bergon," in a matter-of-fact way.

"Pleased to meet your acquaintance. I assume this man is your First Mate."

"He is. First Mate Yu."

"First Mate Yu is an excellent fighter and one of the toughest men I have ever fought in my life. You should be very proud of his effort."

"I am proud of my entire crew, Captain Bergon."

"As am I sir." replied Bergon. "I don't believe any of them are dead yet, though some may be close to death. Whether bleeding out in the hallway or running low on air while floating through space. In the interest of time, please have your crew release three vapor containers and we will be on our way."

"You son of a bitch." Jons grunted. "You attack my crew, board my ship, and then expect me to just roll over and comply."

Bergon stared at Jons and the two shared an intense gaze for several moments. Bergon spoke first, brash and direct. "Captain Jons. You will comply or suffer greater losses than you already have. It really is just that simple."

"Go to hell." Jons replied.

Bergon motioned to one of his crew and the pirate stepped forward and moved over to the logistics section of the bridge. The pirate stood over one of Jons' crew members and declared, "You have been relieved of duty."

The pirate then drove the pickaxe end of her pulaski into the crewman's shoulder and drug them out of their chair. She sat down and began working on the console. A few moments later, red alerts lit up several screens across the bridge, followed by a sudden bump against the hull of the ship.

The pirate stood up, "Capt, the vapor canisters have been released."
Out of the bridge windows, crews aboard both spaceships could see the vapor canisters slowly floating alongside the Prophecy.

"Thank You," Captain Bergon replied. He continued, "Captain Jons, I will collect my three canisters and you can collect your three and proceed to your waypoint. And in the future, you will not regard me with foul language."

Bergon did not mind foul language, but he demanded respect. Especially from those he had conquered.

"In the future," Jons spat. "You will not make it out of here alive pirate."

"You really should know when to quit. You are in no position to resist. You need to rescue your crew, recover your load, and tend to your wounded. Your crew will remember this day forever and yield next time."

"I'll be seeing you shortly, Bergon. Count on it."

Bergon sat Yu in an empty chair and positioned him so that he did not fall. He motioned to his crew and they proceeded toward the bridge door. He stopped short, and with his back to Jons, turned his head slightly to address the angry captain.

"Is it your intention to chase me, Jons?" Bergon slyly asked.

"It is my intention to hunt you down and kill you, Bergon."

"So be it," Bergon replied. He then swiftly turned and with two large strides came back and drove his dagger into Yu's chest. He withdrew the dagger as Yu coughed up blood. The Prophecy bridge crew gasped in horror at the site.

"You will need to get First Mate Yu to a hospital quickly, Jons. He has a punctured lung. I am not in the mood to be hunted today."

Bergon and his crew then departed the bridge and headed back toward the airlock.

Jons rushed over to Yu, removing his jacket to apply pressure to the dagger wound.

"Doc! Get over here. Faaya take the conn! Master Chief Jebel, get a shuttle crew together and rescue our crew." There was panic in Jons' voice. "Navigation, find the closest settlement with a proper hospital."

"Sorry, Captain." Yu murmured. "He was good. I've never seen..."

"Stop talking," Jons interrupted his friend. "Save your strength and tell me later."

Faaya had taken command of the Prophecy and all operations were underway. Master Chief Jebel was boarding the shuttle along with a few crew members to rescue the members in space. A crew member was dispatched to seal the main airlock and another crew member to recover the vapor canisters. The Navigation Section ran through a list of possible destinations.

"Ma'am. Thapus CL1 is a developed settlement with a major hospital. However, there is an outpost on the moon, Prao. They may have a field surgeon on station. We can be on Prao within the hour, Thapus CL1 will take about two hours."

Faaya shouts over the bridge, "Doc, can you keep Yu stable for three hours?"

"I can!" Doc shouted back from behind the console while tending to First Mate Yu.

Faaya stood at the helm "Comm, give me an open channel, all stations."

"Ma'am, your channel is open."

"Attention Prophecy crew. Pirates have damaged our ship and injured our crew. You have 30-minutes to secure the ship, all cargo, and personnel. Take all wounded to medical for care. You now have 29 minutes. Bridge out."

Faaya continued off-air. "Set a course for Thapus CL1. Make sure the engines are not damaged and double-check all exterior seals. Comm, give me a direct line to Jebel's shuttle."

"Ma'am, your line is open," came a reply.

"Master Chief."

"First Mate Faaya."

"You have 20 minutes to get the crew and get back to the Prophecy. We will be taking Yu to Thapus CL1."

"Roger that, ma'am. I will initiate rapid rescue procedures."

"Copy that, Master Chief. Prophecy out."

Jebel placed his helmet back on his head and opened up the side hatch door. He flipped up a red switch cover and pushed the toggle back. Outside the side door, a large rope net unraveled alongside the shuttle. Jebel reached overhead and flipped another switch that activated a blinking red light atop the shuttle.

As the shuttle approached the first stranded crew member, he saw a flashing red light and the rope net flopping on the side of the rescue shuttle. He took a deep breath and braced for impact. Master Chief Jebel steered the shuttle directly at the stranded spacewalker. He then twisted hard on the yoke, causing the shuttle to drift sideways toward the spacewalker. The shuttle slowed for just a moment as it changed direction, but still pushed hard into the spacewalker. The spacewalker absorbed the impact and grabbed hold of the net. The shuttle jerked forward, straining the fingers of the spacewalker as it sped toward the next crew member. The spacewalker used all his strength to pull himself forward along the rope net and into the shuttle bay.

"Holy crap! Things must be bad back at the Prophecy."

"Settle in and brace." Master Chief Jebel replied.

Jebel conducted this maneuver until all crew members were rescued and then sped back to the Prophecy with 3 minutes to spare.

"Jebel to Faaya, all souls on board."

"Roger that, Master Chief. Prepare the shuttle for transport to the planet surface for Yu and other badly wounded personnel."

"Aye, Aye, ma'am."

###

Within 30 minutes of departing the Prophecy, Commander Unadóttir had secured three vapor canisters and was configuring the Black Dagger for transport. The Black Dagger was not initially designed to carry such loads, but was able to do so based on modifications made by Bergon and Vincent. However, carrying loads meant the Black Dagger would not be as fast and agile. This was the primary reason Bergon needed Jons to focus on his crew, and not the Black Dagger. Bergon also knew a wounded crew needed medical attention, while a dead crew did not. If he had killed the Prophecy crew members, including First Mate Yu, nothing would prevent Jons from continuing the fight.

Bergon and Vincent stood on the bridge of the Black Dagger and watched as the two crews, Black Dagger and Prophecy, readied their respective ships for transport. Bergon left the conn of the ship with Commander U, as she was highly skilled in this area of the operation.

"Well, that rescue operation didn't take long." Vincent sounded surprised.

"I think they are in a hurry. I punctured the lung of their First Mate." Bergon responded.

"Well, another non-compliance issue. When are these crews gonna learn?"

"This crew was different Vincent. They were well-disciplined, didn't panic, stayed the course. The First Mate was the best fighter I've ever come across. Captain Jons was unyielding. Honestly, if we didn't know how to operate a Class 9 rig, we wouldn't have gotten the vapor."

"So, you think he would have pursued us?"

"I know he would have. I'm not sure I want to come across his path again."

"Was he that scary?"

"Not scary… just reminded me a lot of myself."

"Now that… is scary."

Commander Unadóttir interrupted, "Captain Bergon, vapor is secure, all crews onboard, and the Black Dagger is ready to set sail. Where to, sir?"

"Standby, Commander U. I want to make sure the Prophecy gets underway before we head out."

"Aye, aye, sir." Unadóttir responded. She then went back to the conduct of the ship.

"You think he's still watching us, Bergon?" Vincent asked quietly.

"I'm not sure. But I don't want to leave any threads for him to tug on either." Bergon spoke softly and intently. Fixated on watching the Prophecy out the bridge window.

###

"Captain Jons. Sir, all personnel are onboard, cargo is secured, and the shuttle is being prepped for surface landing. We have a course set for Thapus CL1." Second Mate Faaya completed the rundown of the Prophecy. "What are your orders, sir?"

"Are the Black Dagger crews still outside?"

"No, sir. They have been buttoned up for a bit now."

"Bergon, you son-of-a-bitch." Jons said under his breath. "Very well, Second Mate Faaya. Set out of Thapus CL1, full speed, but keep an eye on the energy levels."

"Roger that, sir. Engineering, give me full power and let me know if we hit 40%."

"Yes, ma'am," a response came from the Engineering Section.

The Prophecy began to move forward. Slowly at first, it turned right, pitched high, and rotated counterclockwise. Once aligned, the engines began to come to life and the Prophecy continuously increased its speed.

"Doc, move First Mate Yu to the shuttle for transport and make sure he is comfortable for the ride. I'll be done soon." Captain Jons spoke with a caring voice.

"I will, sir." Doc replied. Motioning to the crew members, "You and you, grab the litter and give me a hand." Two crew members grabbed the litter and lifted Yu, while Doc held his IV with one hand and kept pressure on the wound with the other. The three moved with a purpose, yet with extreme care.

Jons walked over to the Watch Leader's console. "Leandro, do you have a fix on the Black Dagger?" Jons spoke in a softer than normal voice. Not necessarily trying to keep others from hearing, but more so to ensure he had Leandro's attention.

"Sir, I've been trying, but the signal keeps dropping. They must have some kind of interference device. Something more advanced than I'm familiar with for sure." Leandro was feverishly working his console.

"Well keep trying. I just want to know the direction they are heading."

"Roger that sir. I'll keep you informed."

Vapor
Episode 2 (*Teaser*)

Thapus CL1

"Prophecy to Base Station Thapus CL1."

"This is Thapus CL1, go for Prophecy."

"This is Prophecy with a medical emergency requesting immediate clearance for shuttle landing."

"State your emergency, Prophecy."

"We have multiple injured from a pirate attack, including a Level 2 lung puncture. Request immediate shuttle docking bay with ground transport standing by."

"Copy that Prophecy; you are clear for immediate docking in shuttle bay 4. Medical ground transport is being coordinated and will meet you on the ground. Will there be anything else, Prophecy?"

"That is all, Thapus CL1; see you in 20 minutes."

"Thapus CL1 out."

Second Mate Faaya brought the Prophecy to orbit around the Thapus CL1 Base Station and Master Chief Jebel finalized the shuttle for ground landing. Using the shuttle for short hops from ship-to-ship in space was different from landing on a planet. Ground landings require additional heat shields and air intake dust guards. Each shuttle on the Prophecy had a ground kit, but they were not left attached. In space, a shuttle with a ground kit attached was slower and less maneuverable. Not by a large variance, but vapor collection was dynamic and a quick and agile shuttle made the process much easier.

"Second Mate Faaya, I'm heading down to the shuttle. I'll be with Yu and the crew at the hospital. While we are down there, see if you can find a buyer for the vapor."

"We will not be taking the vapor to our planned destination, sir?" replied Faaya.

"No, Faaya. We are going to have to alter our plans a bit. Get the best price you can, and run a financial package for me as well."

"Roger that, sir. Is there anything I should know?"

"Not yet, Faaya. For now, let's just get our crew healthy. Check the other wounded to see if anyone else needs ground transport. Send another shuttle if needed. In fact, go ahead and prep a few more shuttles for ground transport and let the crew stretch their legs in short shifts."

"Aye, aye, Captain. I'll get it done."

Faaya returned to the conduct of the ship as Jons moved over to Leandro's workstation.

"Any luck?" Jons inquired.

"No, sir. They didn't budge." Leandro responded. "It's like they knew we were watching. But I've got a few ideas, Captain. I'll have something for you when you return to the ship."

"I may be down there for a while. How much time do you need?"

"A few hours."

"OK, I'll buzz after the crew is settled in the hospital. And Leandro…I want that bastard."

Concept Art

As part of my Vapor series, I will be creating an entire new world. A world located in the future. A future of space exploration.

Since I will be dealing with space, I am going to need space suits. The first part of creating new art is pulling reference material. The space suits sketched below are based on real world and movie space suits. So I will not be using them directly. But I will be using them to generate new ideas.

I will need a few different types of suits. I will need suits for military, merchants, mercs, pirates, and civilians. This should be fun.

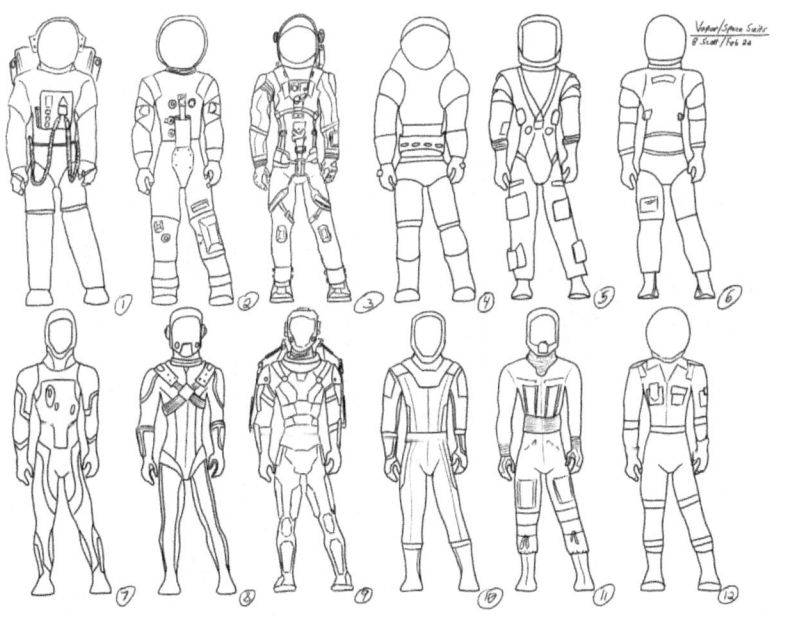

Here I am taking a closer look at the Prophecy crew. Their space suits are built for working outside for extended periods of time.

It's important to look at the design details, as well as, the silhouette.

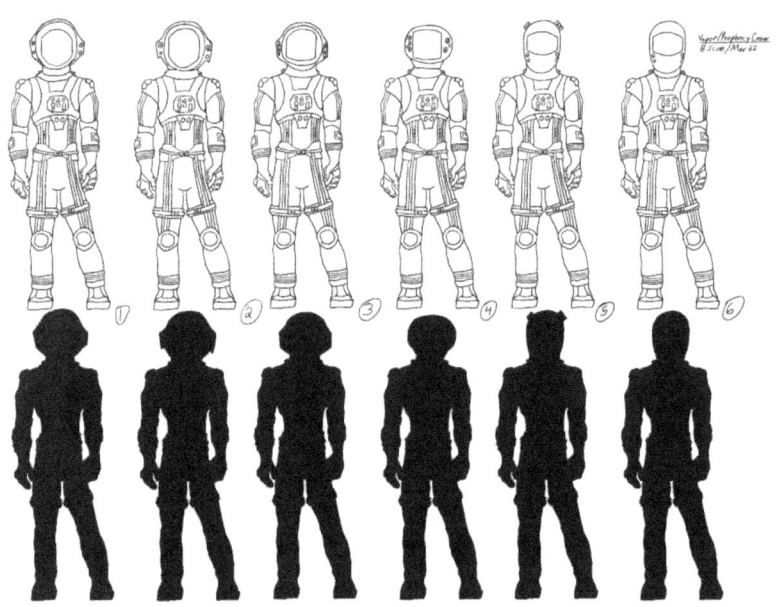

Next, I start working on the Black Dagger crew space suits. The pirate space suits are built for fighting. Mobility and dexterity are important.

The silhouette should be easily distinguishable from the Prophecy.

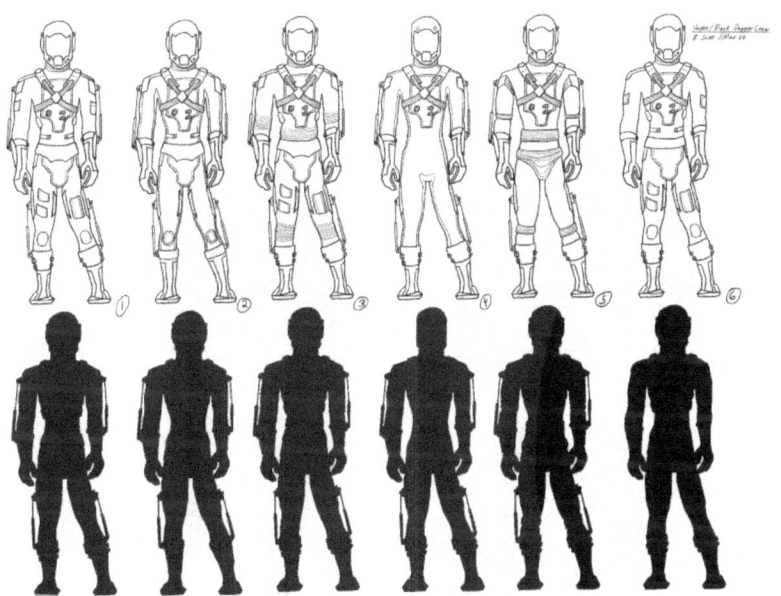

I work with a team of artists to get feedback on the final designs. With some tweaks back and forth, I get a pair of really nice silhouettes. The Prophecy work crew are big and bulky, compared to the slim Black Dagger pirates. Even without the line details, you can easily recognize each from one another.

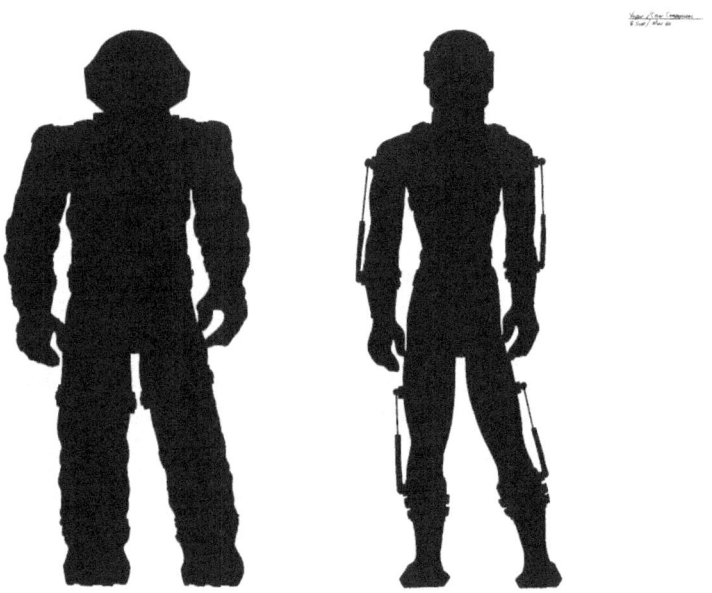

48

Finally, the line details. However, this is not the last step. Each crew member needs gear. Tools, weapons, personal items, etc. I'll explore these more in the next book.

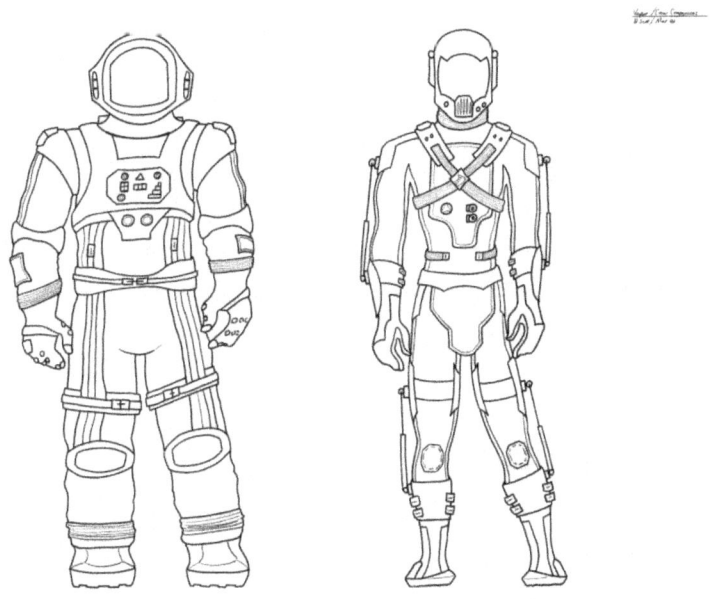

This book made possible by the support of:

Amy Stark
Brian Lue Sang
Brian Williams
Bryan Dempsey
Caitlin Wilks
Carissa Falco
Chris Dixon
Chris Elam
Cory Pawlicki
Crazy1afro
Dominic Giambra
Dragonsteel Entertainment
drjsperkins
Eric Hansen

Eron Wyngarde
Frank Fedele
Hunter Jeske
Jacqui Mae Hencsie
Jaimie Engle
Jason Burgos
Jason Woulas

Jeffrey Kulisek
Joel Quinn
Joseph Weisensee
JPescatore
Kane
Kathryn Schmidt
Kesley Woodard
Kurt Beyerl
Lorme Jourdan
Michael Harvey
Nick Greenup
Peter Pappas
Roel Mulder
The Creative Fund by
BackerKit

About Brad Scott

Brad Scott is an artist, illustrator, storyteller, author, conceptual art designer, game designer, and engineer. His art works include traditional and digital media. His written works include short stories, novels, tabletop role-playing games, comics, and movie scripts. His blended style allows him to share art and storytelling in unique ways.

www.ingramcontent.com/pod-product-compliance
Lightning Source LLC
Chambersburg PA
CBHW070810120626
46557CB00002B/803